HURRY UP!

A Book About Slowing Down

written by

Kate Dopirak

illustrated by

Christopher Silas Neal

Bookroo

Hurry up!

Hurry down.

Hurry round and round . . .

and round.

Hurry here.

Hurry there.

Hurry, scurry *everywhere!*

Hurry out.

Hurry in.

Hurry if you want to win.

Hurry so you'll reach the **top.**

Hurry

Hurry

Hurry

Slow things down.

Take a break.

Look around, for goodness' sake.

Breathe it in.

Blow it out.

This is what it's all about.

Make a wish.

Take a walk.

Listen to the forest talk.

Go explore.
Make new friends.

Find out where the rainbow ends.

Count the stars,
easy does.

Marvel at the nighttime buzz.

Mosey home.

Stretch and yawn.

Race is off,
and rest is on.

No more fast—
slooooooow instead.

Dreams and lazy days ahead.

For Joey and Bobby, my inspiration—K. D.

For Jasper and River:
don't forget to slow down every now and then—C. S. N.

Bookroo

Bookroo, 971 S University Dr #1020, Provo, UT 84601
Create a beautiful home library with Bookroo's book clubs. Join at www.bookroo.com.

Originally published by Beach Lane Books,
An imprint of Simon & Schuster Children's Publishing Division
1230 Avenue of the Americas, New York, NY 10020

Book design by Lauren Rille
The text for this book was set in Brandon Grotesque.
The illustrations for this book were rendered in mixed media.

Spine design by Bookroo
First Bookroo Edition, 2022
ISBN: 978-1-955899-39-0
10 9 8 7 6 5 4 3 2 1